FEB 1 8 2011

CAPITAL AREA DISTRICT LIBRARY
DISCARD
CADL

SHARK ZONE

HAMMERHEAD SHARK

by Jody Sullivan Rake

Reading Consultant:
Barbara J. Fox
Reading Specialist
North Carolina State University

Content Consultant:
Deborah Nuzzolo
Education Manager
SeaWorld, San Diego

CAPSTONE PRESS
a capstone imprint

Blazers is published by Capstone Press,
151 Good Counsel Drive, P.O. Box 669, Mankato, Minnesota 56002.
www.capstonepub.com

Copyright © 2011 by Capstone Press, a Capstone imprint.
All rights reserved.
No part of this publication may be reproduced in whole or in part, or stored in a retrieval system, or transmitted in any form or by any means, electronic, mechanical, photocopying, recording, or otherwise, without written permission of the publisher.
For information regarding permission, write to Capstone Press,
151 Good Counsel Drive, P.O. Box 669, Dept. R, Mankato, Minnesota 56002.

 Books published by Capstone Press are manufactured with paper containing at least 10 percent post-consumer waste.

Library of Congress Cataloging-in-Publication Data
Rake, Jody Sullivan.
　Hammerhead shark / by Jody Sullivan Rake.
　　p. cm.—(Blazers. Shark zone)
　Includes bibliographical references and index.
　Summary: "Describes the hammerhead shark, including physical features, habitat, hunting, and role in the ecosystem"—Provided by publisher.
　ISBN 978-1-4296-5014-4 (library binding)
　1. Hammerhead sharks—Juvenile literature. I. Title. II. Series.

QL638.95.S7R35 2011
597.3'4—dc22
　　　　　　　　　　　　　　　　　2010002271

Editorial Credits
Lori Shores, editor; Juliette Peters, designer; Kelly Garvin, media researcher;
　Laura Manthe, production specialist

Photo Credits
Alamy/Brandon Cole, 16–17
Jeff Rotman, 12, 14–15, 22–23
Seapics/David B. Fleetham, 10–11; Doug Perrine, 27; James D. Watt, cover, 9, 24–25;
　Masa Ushioda, 5, 6–7, 19, 21, 28–29
Shutterstock/artida; Eky Chan; Giuseppe_R, design elements

Essential content terms are **bold** and are defined on the page where they first appear.

Printed in the United States of America in Stevens Point, Wisconsin.
092010
005957R

TABLE OF CONTENTS

Chapter 1 **On the Hunt**	4
Chapter 2 **A Head for Hunting**	8
Chapter 3 **Hammerhead Homes**	20
Chapter 4 **Hammerheads and Humans**	26
Glossary	30
Read More	31
Internet Sites	31
Index	32

CHAPTER 1

ON THE HUNT

A long, slender shark swims along the ocean floor. It sweeps back and forth with its weird T-shaped head. Its wide eyes keep watch over large areas of sand.

The shark senses a tiny movement under the sand. Its head whips toward a startled stingray. The hammerhead shark has found its **prey**.

SHARK FACT

Hammerheads are dangerous animals. But very few hammerhead attacks have been recorded.

prey—an animal hunted by another animal for food

CHAPTER 2

A HEAD FOR HUNTING

A hammerhead's broad, flat head is perfect for finding prey. Its head is covered with tiny pinholes. These **sense organs** feel the electrical energy made by other animals' movements.

sense organ—a body part that sends messages to the brain

SHARK FACT

The hammerhead's sense organs only work at close range. The shark must be just a few inches away to feel its prey.

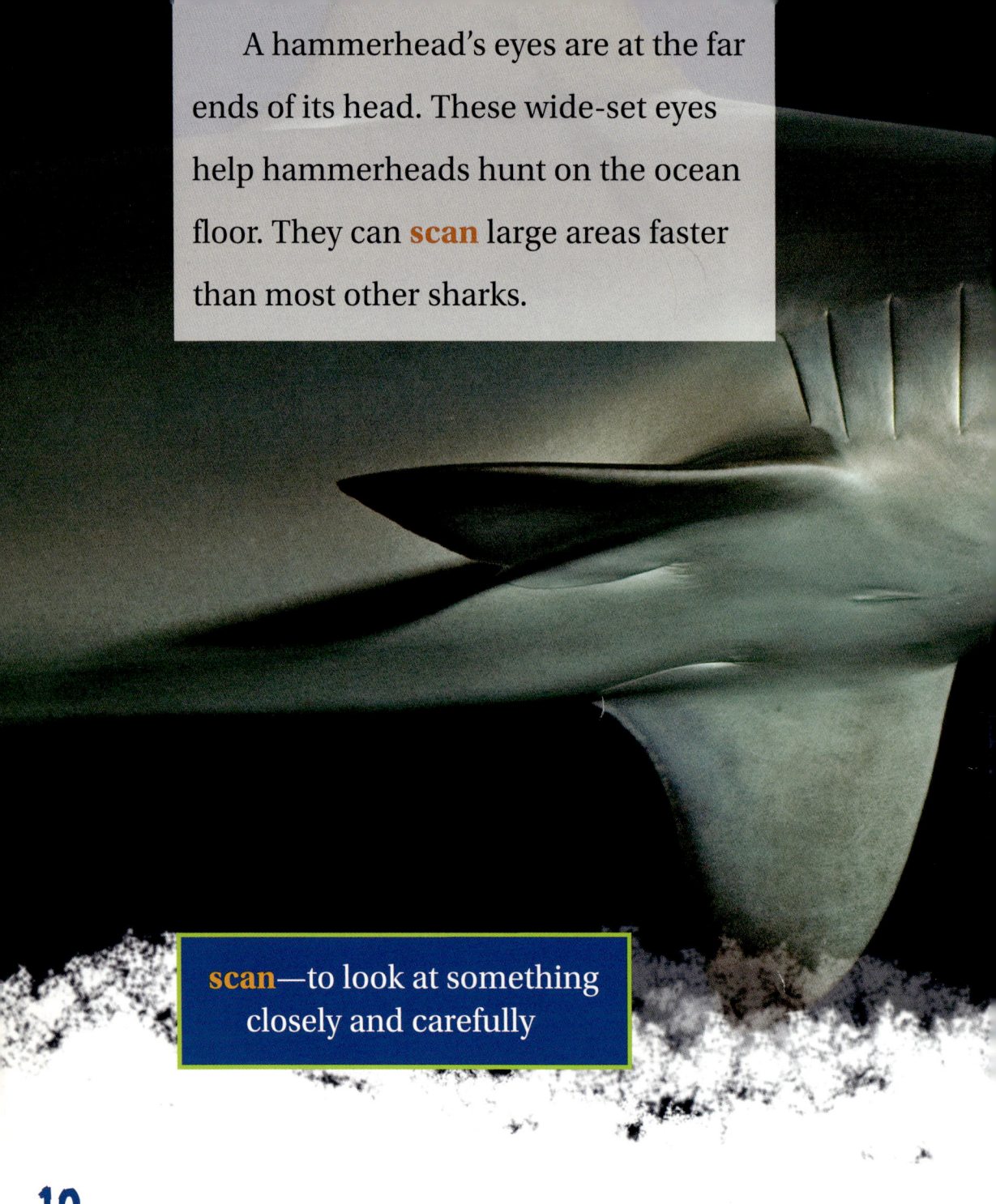

A hammerhead's eyes are at the far ends of its head. These wide-set eyes help hammerheads hunt on the ocean floor. They can **scan** large areas faster than most other sharks.

scan—to look at something closely and carefully

eye

SHARK FACT

A hammerhead's nose openings are also on the far ends of its head.

Hammerheads usually feed on the bottom of the sea. They mainly eat stingrays. These **predators** also hunt fish, squid, and **shellfish**.

SHARK FACT

Hammerheads use their broad heads to pin down prey.

predator—an animal that hunts other animals for food

shellfish—a sea creature with a shell, such as a shrimp, crab, or lobster

A hammerhead shark's mouth is underneath its head. The hammerhead scoops up prey with its small mouth. It tears the prey apart with its many sharp, jagged teeth.

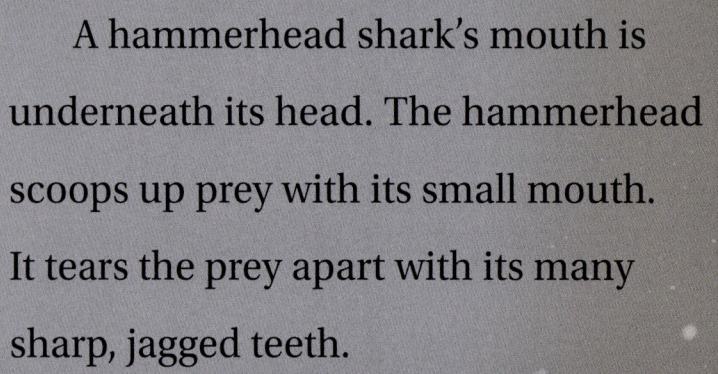

SHARK FACT

Hammerhead sharks have triangle-shaped teeth.

A hammerhead's rocket-shaped body glides smoothly through the water. Its **tail fin** is longer on the top than on the bottom. This feature gives the shark more power to swim down to the ocean floor.

tail fin top

tail fin bottom

tail fin—the hard, flat body part at the tail end of a shark

17

Nine kinds of hammerheads swim in the oceans. The great hammerhead is the largest. It grows up to 20 feet (6 meters) long. Most hammerheads are between 11 and 13 feet (3.4 and 4 meters) long.

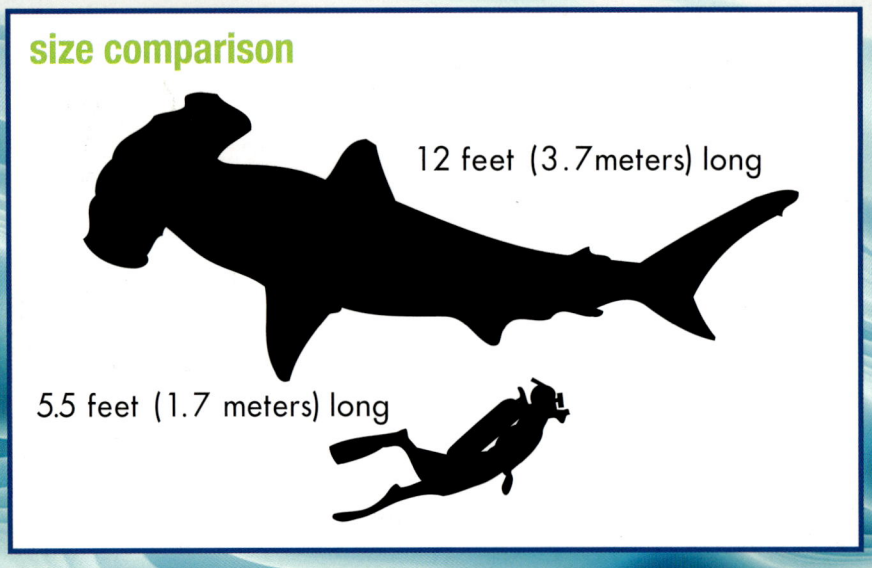

SHARK FACT

The bonnethead is the smallest hammerhead shark. It measures just under 5 feet (1.5 meters) in length.

bonnethead shark

CHAPTER 3
HAMMERHEAD HOMES

Hammerheads live in warm **temperate** and tropical seas around the world. Large hammerheads swim in deep waters. Small hammerheads stick to sheltered coastlines.

temperate—an area that has neither very high nor very low temperatures

Hammerhead Sharks Range

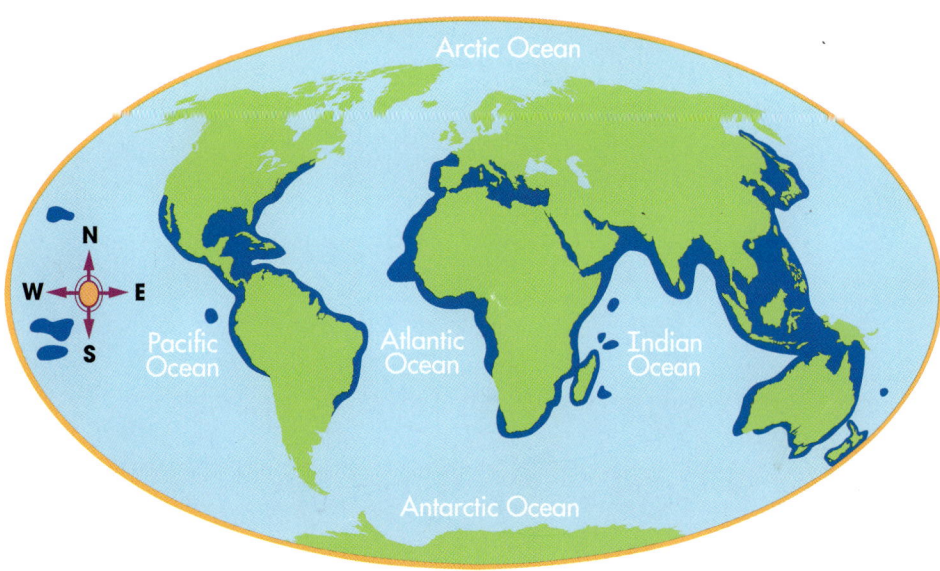

where hammerhead sharks live

In summer months, hammerhead sharks move to cooler waters. They travel in groups that sometimes number in the hundreds.

SHARK FACT

Scientists believe hammerheads find their way using magnetic fields on the ocean floor.

Hammerheads help keep the ocean **ecosystem** healthy. They control stingray and other animal populations that live on the ocean floor.

ecosystem—a group of animals and plants that work together with their surroundings

SHARK FACT

Hammerheads don't compete with other large sharks for food. Instead they hunt on the ocean floor.

CHAPTER 4

HAMMERHEADS AND HUMANS

Hammerhead sharks look scary, but they hardly ever attack people. They may bite when they feel threatened. But most hammerhead bites are not serious.

SHARK FACT

Each year, thousands of hammerhead sharks become tangled in fishing nets and die.

Some human activities are dangerous for hammerheads. People hunt these sharks for sport and for food. But **conservation** groups are working to make laws that protect hammerhead sharks.

conservation—the protection of valuable things, especially forests, wildlife, and natural resources

Glossary

conservation (kon-sur-VAY-shuhn)—the protection of valuable things, especially forests, wildlife, and natural resources

ecosystem (EE-koh-sis-tuhm)—a group of animals and plants that work together with their surroundings

magnetic field (mag-NET-ik FEELD)—an area in the earth that has the power to attract some metals

predator (PRED-uh-tor)—an animal that hunts other animals for food

prey (PRAY)—an animal hunted by another animal for food

scan (SKAN)—to look at something closely and carefully

sense organ (SENSS OR-guhn)—a body part that sends messages to the brain

shellfish (SHEL-fish)—a sea creature with a shell, such as a shrimp, crab, lobster, or mussel

tail fin (TAYL FIN)—the hard, flat body part at the tail end of a shark

temperate (TEM-pur-it)—an area that has neither very high nor very low temperatures

Read More

Berman, Ruth. *Sharks.* Nature Watch. Minneapolis: Lerner Publications, 2009.

O'Donnell, Kerri. *Hammerhead Sharks.* Ugly Animals. New York: PowerKids Press, 2007.

Randolph, Joanne. *The Hammerhead Shark: Coastal Killer.* Sharks: Hunters of the Deep. New York: Powerkids Press, 2007.

Smith, Miranda. *Sharks.* Kingfisher Knowledge. New York: Kingfisher, 2008.

Internet Sites

FactHound offers a safe, fun way to find Internet sites related to this book. All of the sites on FactHound have been researched by our staff.

Here's all you do:

Visit *www.facthound.com*

FactHound will fetch the best sites for you!

Index

bites, 26
bodies, 16

eating, 13, 14
ecosystems, 24
eyes, 4, 10

fins, 16
fishing nets, 28

groups, 22

habitat, 20
heads, 4, 6, 8, 10, 13
hunting, 6, 8, 10

mouths, 14

people, 26, 28
predators, 13
prey, 6, 8, 13, 14, 24
protecting hammerheads, 28

range, 20

sense organs, 8
size, 6, 18
species of hammerheads, 18

teeth, 14